panda series

PANDA books are for first readers beginning to make their own way through books.

My Dog Lively

PATRICK DEELEY

 • Pictures by Martin Fagan •

THE O'BRIEN PRESS
DUBLIN

First published 2001 by The O'Brien Press Ltd,
12 Terenure Road East, Rathgar, Dublin 6, Ireland.
Tel: +353 1 4923333; Fax: +353 1 4922777
E-mail: books@obrien.ie
Website: www.obrien.ie
Reprinted 2002, 2003, 2007.

ISBN: 978-0-86278-723-3

British Library Cataloguing-in-Publication Data
Deeley, Patrick, 1953-
My dog Lively. - (Pandas ; 19)
1.Dogs - Juvenile fiction 2.Children's stories
I.Title II.Fagan, Martin
823.9'14[J]

The O'Brien Press receives assistance from

4 5 6 7
07 08 09 10 11

Typesetting, layout, editing, design: The O'Brien Press Ltd
Printing: Cox & Wyman Ltd

For Genevieve

Can YOU spot the panda
hidden in the story?

'I'm six! I'm six today!'
Jenny shouted,
jumping up and down
on her bed.

Jenny's toy dogs
bounced and danced with her.

Jenny loved her dogs.
There was one
for each birthday.

The dalmatian
did a somersault.

The cocker spaniel
flapped its long, silken ears.

The golden retriever
flew out of its wicker basket.

The sheepdog fell on its tail.

The plastic terrier on wheels
rolled onto the floor
with a loud crash.

Then it moved away,
letting out a single 'Yap'.

'I have five dogs,' said Jenny,
'one for each birthday.
I wonder what kind of dog
I'll get this time?'

She ran downstairs
to the kitchen.
Her gifts were all wrapped
and waiting for her
on the table.

She got books and cards
and a doll –
and a leather dog collar!
It had a shiny buckle
and a name-tag, made of silver,
that winked in the
morning sunlight.

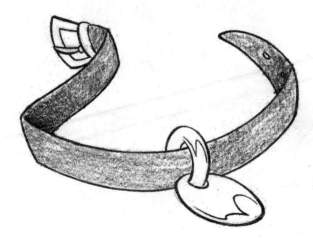

'Who's this for?' said Jenny.

'Look!' smiled Mum.

And there at the glass door,

his front paws on the step,

was a little collie,

staring in at Jenny.

'A real dog at last!' Jenny said.
'This is the best birthday ever.'

The collie jumped up
and bumped her on the nose.

He was wildly excited.
He wagged his tail so hard
it slapped at Jenny's legs.

He ran round and round
in circles.

He rolled and leaped
and danced among the daisies.

He barked at
the neighbour's cat.

He snapped at
a swarm of bees,
busy in the honeysuckle hedge.

He chased.

He tumbled.

He spun.

That dog just
could not stay still.

'I'll call you Lively,' Jenny said.
She threw a stick to
the far end of the garden.
'Run, Lively. Get the stick!'
she shouted.

Lively didn't need
to be told twice.
He charged after the stick.

He rolled in the earth
with the stick between his paws.
He tossed it in the air
and caught it as it fell.

Then he looked at Jenny.
'Give me the stick,' Jenny said.

But Lively wouldn't bring it.
She had to chase him
around the laurel bushes,
through the rockery flowers,
and back by the garden path.

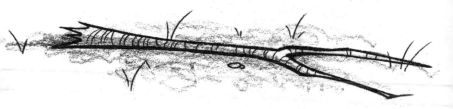

At last, Lively dropped the stick.

After breakfast,
Jenny and Mum went to buy
a kennel for Lively.
It was made of wood.
They put it in the back garden.

'Lively,' said Jenny,
'this is your own little house.'

But Lively didn't even look at it.
He just wanted to play ...

'A brisk walk will tire him out,'
said Mum later.
She had bought a lead for him.
She showed Jenny
how to clip the lead
to Lively's collar.

Then Jenny strapped the collar
around his neck.

But Lively didn't want to walk.
He wanted to **fly**.
He tugged at his lead
every step of the way.

Jenny had to run to keep up.
She dashed around the park.

Lively saw some ducks
in the duck-pond.
He dived straight in
and nearly pulled Jenny
with him.
The ducks flew to
their little island
in the middle of the pond.

Jenny hauled Lively out,
and he shook the water off,
all over her!

Then they raced through
the woods near the park.
Lively caught sight
of a squirrel and gave chase,
pulling Jenny with him.
The squirrel ran up a tree.

Mum came to find them.
'I think Lively's had enough
exercise for one day,' she said.

'I hope so,' said Jenny.
'I'm exhausted.'

That evening,
Jenny crawled into the kennel
to show Lively it was
time for bed.
It was snug and cosy inside.

But Lively wouldn't go in.
He whimpered
and licked Jenny's face.
'Can he sleep in my room?'
Jenny asked.
'No,' Mum said.
'He must learn to sleep
in his own little house.'

'He's afraid of the dark,'
Jenny said.
'We'll turn his kennel
towards the house,' Mum said.
'He'll see the light
in the kitchen window.'

'But he's **lonely**,' said Jenny.
'We'll give him
your old rag doll,' said Mum.

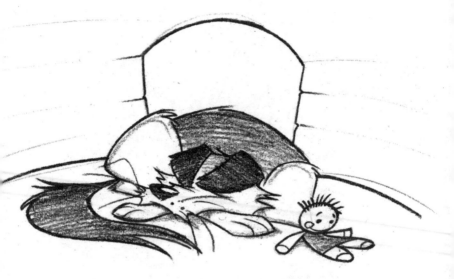

In the end, Lively was happy
to stay in his kennel.
He slept in the shape of a circle.

'**Food**' and '**Walk**' were
Lively's two favourite words.
Each time he heard them,
he would lift his ears
and cock his head.

Jenny showed him her toy dogs.
He loved to run beside
the yapping terrier on wheels
as Jenny pushed it along.

But he chewed the
cocker spaniel's ear.

He buried the
golden retriever's
pretend bone.

'Oh no!' said Jenny. 'Bad dog!'
But when he whimpered,
she always forgave him.

During the long summer days
Jenny and Lively played
tug-of-war with sticks,
and games of hide-and-seek
among the shrubs.

And each night
Jenny fell into bed, exhausted.

One day Jenny fell and
scraped her knees badly.
Lively ran to the house
and barked loudly
until Mum heard him.

'You're my **best friend**,' Jenny told him later.

He gazed into her eyes
to let her know that she was
his **best friend** too.

But next day
Lively dug a big hole
in the middle of
Mum's lovely lawn.

Then he snapped
at the sunflower stalks,
and the golden flowerheads
toppled to the ground.
Mum was very sad.

When Lively tugged the sheets
from the clothesline
and wrestled with them
in the mud,
Mum was **furious**.
'Bold dog!' she shouted.

'I'm fed up,' said Jenny.
'Why is Lively so naughty?'
'He's a young dog,' said Mum.
'We must try to be
patient with him.
He'll get better, you'll see.'

But Lively got **worse**.
He ran and raced
all over the house.

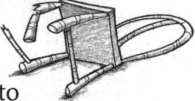

He crashed into
tables and chairs,
he was in such a hurry.

He munched on everything.

He chewed his kennel door.

'We'll have to train Lively,'
said Mum, and Jenny agreed.
They took him to a
school for dogs.

Lively sniffed at the other dogs.
And they sniffed at him.

He barked
at a curly poodle.

He growled
at a golden spaniel.

When he saw a huge labrador,
Lively bared his teeth
and gave a low, nasty growl.

The labrador growled back!

The instructor gathered
the dogs and their owners
in a large circle.
'An obedient dog
is a happy dog,' she said.

She took Lively's lead.
'Heel,' she said,
holding him close to her.
He tried to pull away
but she jerked him back.
'**Heel**,' she said again.

After a very long time
Lively walked beside her –
for a while.
She praised him
and gave him a treat.
'Now you try, Jenny,' she said.

Lively's ears perked up.
His eyes twinkled.
'Oh no,' said Jenny.
'He's going to be
troublesome.'

And he was.

In the end,
he tugged the lead
out of Jenny's hand
and ran away from school!

It took weeks and weeks
to get Lively to walk properly.
But one day he did it.
Lively walked.

(Well, while he was at school.)

All the other dog owners
gave Jenny and Lively
a great big cheer.

'At last,' said Mum,
'Lively is a good dog.'
'He's as **good** as **gold**,'
said Jenny.

But he wasn't!
When they looked
out the window,
he was digging a new hole!

Lively was always lively.

He always dug holes.

He always crashed into things.

He barked at cats.

He ate Mum's flowers.

He chewed Jenny's toy dogs.

He tore her schoolbooks.

Lively was **trouble**.

Always.

But he was Jenny's own dog
and she loved him to bits.
'Mad dog,' she'd say.
'Silly billy!'

And Lively loved Jenny too
in his own wild way.

Just before Jenny's
seventh birthday,
Mum asked her
what she would like.
'I'd really love a bear,'
Jenny said.

Then she looked at Lively.

'Just as long as it's not
a real **live** bear!'
she said.